Mix-Up Monday

An original concept by author Elizabeth Dale

© Elizabeth Dale

Illustrated by Louise Forshaw

MAVERICK ARTS PUBLISHING LTD

Studio 11, City Business Centre, 6 Brighton Road, Horsham,
West Sussex, RH13 5BB, +44 (0)1403 256941

© Maverick Arts Publishing Limited

Published July 2021

A CIP catalogue record for this book
is available at the British Library.

ISBN 978-1-84886-640-9

LONDON BOROUGH OF RICHMOND UPON THAMES	
90710 000 481 569	
Askews & Holts	30-Jul-2021
JF	
RTCA	

DISCARDED FROM RICHMOND UPON THAMES LIBRARY SERVICE

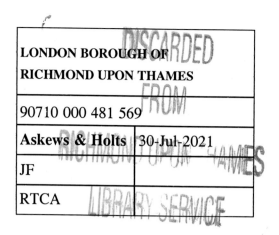

Maverick publishing

www.maverickbooks.co.uk

For my wonderful, kind friend, Bee,
in memory of all the many mixed-up
Mondays! With much love – E.D.

For Isabella, with love from your favourite Auntie – L.F.

MIX-UP MONDAY

Written by
Elizabeth Dale

Illustrated by
Louise Forshaw

On Monday morning, Farmer Fred wakes from a bad night's sleep.

"Oh no!" he yells, "It's **late!** I have to feed my cows and sheep!"

But he is still so sleepy as he starts to wash and dress.

Can YOU see what he's doing wrong...

...and why he looks a mess?

Fred hurries to the kennel, calling, "Come on quick, young Ben!"
But opens up the hen-house door – and lets out Betsy Hen!

His flock of sheep and little lambs all see that something's wrong,

And think, 'It's Mix-up Monday, so we'd better play along!'

"Good morning, sheep!" the farmer calls, "Now, tell me how are you?"

Well, can you guess what they reply? Together, they all...

So sleepy Fred then shakes his head and wipes his eyes and blinks,

'If they all moo, they must be cows!'

the tired farmer thinks.

He leads them through a doorway and the sheep all get a shock

To find they're in the parlour... and Fred tries to **milk** his flock!

"No milk today?" says Farmer Fred and leads them all away,

Then calling to his horses says, "How are you all today?"

The three brown mares all canter up, so eager for a snack

And having heard the sheep all moo, together they all...

QUACK!

So sleepy Fred then shakes his head and wipes his eyes and blinks,

'If they all **quack**, they must be **ducks!**' the tired farmer thinks.

'I'll have to find some nice **duck eggs**.' But as he reaches down,

He says, "These eggs are **smelly** and it's strange that they are **brown**!"

As Farmer Fred walks on, his **donkeys** rush towards the gate.

"I'm here at last," the farmer cries. "So sorry that I'm late."

And as he strokes their thick long coats, he asks them how they are,

And having heard the horses **quack**, together they call...

BAAAAA!

So sleepy Fred then shakes his head and wipes his eyes and blinks,

'If they all **baa**, they must be **sheep**!' the tired farmer thinks.

'Their coats are far too **thick** so I must shear their **wool** today.'

But the first one doesn't like it – and the others run away!

"Come back you **sheep!**" the farmer calls. "Oh, round them up please, Ben!"

He quickly blows his whistle and off scurries Betsy Hen.

The cows all see, they call HEE-HAW!

The ducks and chicks cry NEIGH!

But Fred still doesn't realise he's had a mixed-up day!

Fred wanders back to see his cows who'd made the donkey sound,

And, yawning, thinks 'Why should I walk when I can ride around?'

He slowly climbs the big, old gate, then throws himself on Daisy.

She's never had a rider on her back - and thinks it's crazy!

"Whoa, slow down, donkey!" Fred commands - well that makes Daisy moo!
She's not a donkey, she's a cow - and proud to be one too!

She twists and turns to shake Fred off, she races here and there,

And then she stops! And suddenly...

The ducklings see him coming and they hide quick as a flash,

But Fred goes flying overhead and lands with such a...

SPLASH!

The **shock** has woken Fred at last, he shakes his head and blinks,
Then realises how he's dressed and what the farmyard thinks!

"It's Mix-up Monday, isn't it?" he calls to everyone.

"I'm glad it's halfway over and you've had your mixed-up fun!"

He smiles and says, "Tomorrow I'll have such a **lovely** snooze-day!"

Forgetting Mix-up Monday leads to...

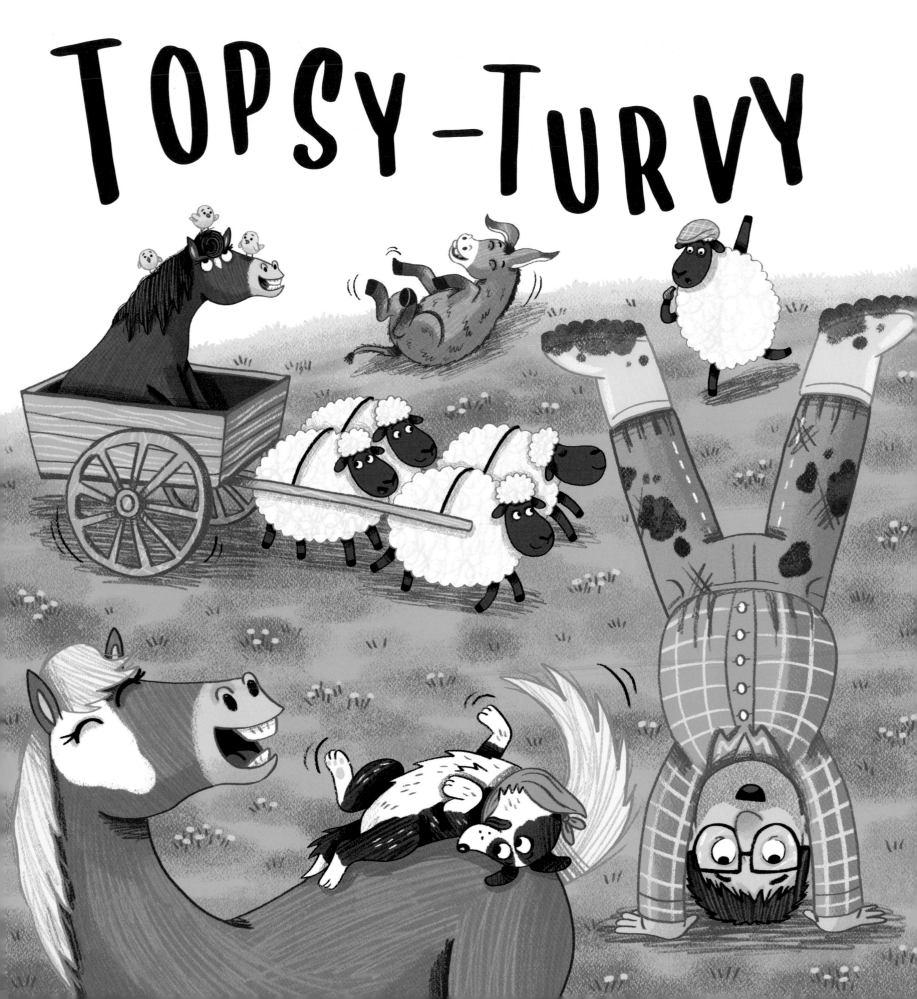